I0624594

Stone
&Iris

Stone & Iris

a short story by
JONATHAN BALLAGH

Stone & Iris

Copyright © 2016 by Jonathan Ballagh

ISBN: 978-0-9967138-3-2 (print)
ISBN: 978-0-9967138-2-5 (ebook)

All rights reserved.

Edited by David Gatewood
www.lonetrout.com

Cover design by Ben J. Adams
www.benjadams.com

This is a work of fiction. Names, characters, businesses, places, events and incidents are either the products of the author's imagination or used in a fictitious manner. Any resemblance to actual persons, living or dead, or actual events is purely coincidental.

To Lisa

Chapter One

MEMORIES ARE CURIOUS THINGS. We mistake them for perfect copies of life; experiences etched in crystal and tucked away for later. But they change on us when we least expect it. A detail is forgotten and a new reality scabs over the hole. History is scarred, the story reimagined. And the strange thing is we don't even realize it's happening. It just does.

This memory is different though. It's special because it's my first: pale sand against a paler sky, the sun struggling through clouds left from a storm the night before. My parents sat together on the beach. Discussing life. Too distracted to notice their three-year-old daughter walking across the sand and into the surf.

It was too late when I turned around, searching desperately for a familiar face among the umbrellas. I remember the pull of the ocean that took hold and carried me out farther still, the wave that crested over my head, the undertow that kept me down. Those long moments below when all things stopped, until a hand plunged through the surface and brought me up.

And then, the greatest breath of my life.

"Alison! Don't ever—" Dad scolded before he raised me up and held me close. I locked my arms around his neck and wept into his hair. Only when he didn't let go, when I felt my wet cheek against his, did I feel safe again. Staring back over his shoulder at the unforgiving churn, I knew that one day I would be gone. But the waves, steady and relentless, they were forever.

Until they weren't. Now they are just memories.

Almost forty years later, as I stand in the water, the ocean has finally lost its breath. The sea is dark and still: a mirror that reflects a forest of shimmering limbs. So many others around me, wherever there is enough space to stand and the water is shallow. All of us crowded together in a line that vanishes along the coast.

And for once, no one is staring down at tiny screens, trying to be somewhere else.

They stare up, instead. Waiting as it draws near, pushing us back into the water. The sky, naked without cloud, is otherwise beautiful—but that's not what they see. They see the part of the sky that is missing altogether. They see a rift, darker than night, and emptier too, stretched wide and jagged like raven wings that eclipse the day.

They see the pieces of the horizon that flicker like a candle.

Extinguished like a candle.

Billion-year-old atoms wiped out, their histories erased, like they never existed.

And maybe they never did.

Chapter Two

I PUSHED THE BUTTON and watched the taillights from the cab fade into the snowfall.

"Yes?" a voice crackled back through the wall speaker.

"Hello? It's Dr. Shaw. Alison Shaw. I had an appointment with Professor Murphy. I know it's almost midnight, but he said—"

"Just a second," the voice interrupted.

A click, and the glass doors slid open. I brushed the snow off my coat and stepped inside. The warm air hit my face at once, providing relief from the cold.

"Sorry I'm late," I called out, my luggage scraping across the lobby floor. A young man sat behind the reception desk and his face was hidden behind a screen. He didn't bother looking up.

Ignoring the lack of hospitality, I pressed on. "I was asked to come straight over as soon as my flight landed, and I got here as fast as I could. The storm wreaked havoc at the airport and—"

"You're already in the system," the receptionist replied curtly. His fingers rattled across the keys. "Welcome to the Human Cognition Research Campus, Dr. Shaw. Professor Murphy is expecting you. His office is down the hall." He stopped typing and gestured with a gnawed pen. "Second door on the right. Hold on a second. Smile on the count of three. One... Two..." He clicked the mouse, the room flashed, and a printer whirred to life under the desk. Seconds later, he fanned a glossy photo back and forth before sliding it into a plastic case.

"For you," he said, looking up at last and pushing the badge across the desk. "Wear it at all times and just swipe it against the scanner. If you end up sticking around, it'll get you in and out of the building too. You can leave your coat and luggage here." His eyes darted back to the screen, letting me know our conversation was over.

I made my way down the hall as directed. The professor bounded to life when I entered his office. "Dr. Shaw, thank you so much for coming. Very nice to meet you." A hand lunged forward from a short, sinewy frame. Trimmed gray hair flanked a balding head and a thick mustache nearly covered his smile. He had a kind face that reminded me of someone I once knew, but couldn't recall.

"Don't mention it, professor," I replied, returning his grip. "When we spoke on the phone, you said you needed me here urgently—some kind of emergency."

"Yes, I can't tell you how much I appreciate it. I realize you had to drop everything to come here. After we talk, I hope you'll agree your trip was worth it. Because there's something I need to show you. Something you must see. But first, there's this…"

The professor paused before handing me a sheet of paper brimming with fine print. "Standard non-disclosure agreement, Dr. Shaw. All you have to do is sign your life away." He laughed apprehensively and turned to face a frosty window that overlooked the research center. The snow fell fast, and the lights from the university buildings collected in amber pools on the drifts. "Please. Take as much time as you need."

Too exhausted to read the details, I signed. The professor relaxed as soon as the paper was back safely in his hand. He took a seat at his desk and motioned for me to do the same.

"Okay. Why don't we start with what you already know about what we do here?"

"I'm no expert, Professor Mur—"

"Please, call me David."

"Okay, David. Like I was saying, I'm no expert, but I've tried to keep up—as much as I can, at least. I know the end goal is to simulate the human brain. The entire brain. The very definition of big science."

I hesitated for a moment, but then continued. "Of course, the media doesn't exactly portray your project in the most positive light." It had been reported that billions of taxpayer dollars had been spent with not a lot to show for it. Most neuroscientists had written the idea off as infeasible, a boondoggle. And in the last year alone, the professor had lost three quarters of his staff. I wasn't sure whether to think of this project as wildly ambitious or a colossal waste of resources.

David looked away from me and stared at a framed picture on his desk. In it, I could see his face from the side and possibly two others, though the angle made it difficult to discern. When he saw where my gaze had fallen, he adjusted the photo slightly so that the other faces remained out of sight. His action struck me as odd, but it was late and I was tired. I quickly forgot about it when the professor smiled.

"I've read the media reports," he said. "But can you reserve judgment until you hear me out? The press isn't exactly in tune with everything going on here."

I fidgeted a bit. Noticing my unease, he continued, "Lots of great science has come from this."

"Such as?"

"For starters, our team has made substantial contributions to neuroscience. No longer are researchers working in the dark when it comes to brain disease. We've helped push forward state-of-the-art treatments for several progressive neurodegenerative disorders. As far as I'm concerned, those advancements alone have made this research worthwhile. You can't put a price on that."

I nodded.

"But there's also these." He opened the desk drawer and removed a handful of devices no larger than postage stamps, and almost as thin.

"Neuromorphic chips," the professor said, spreading the silicon across the desk.

"Circuits that model neural pathways," I added. "Impressive technology, but they've been around for a while now."

"That's true, but you might not believe just how far they've advanced with our research guiding them. Each one of these"—he held a chip up and twisted it until the light caught the edge—"can simulate millions of neurons. At first, these devices provided only crude approximations of brain structures, but now…"

He took a breath and considered the design. "Now they're based on a new architecture that almost perfectly matches their biological equivalent. This is about as close to the real thing as it gets."

I watched intently as his focus shifted back to the drawer. "We're also working to help the blind," David continued, retrieving a metallic sphere and handing it to me. It was silver and gold, with thin layers of glass in front and a bundle of wires extruding from the back. "That's an artificial eye you're holding—the state of the art in visual prosthetics. This project has become especially important to us," he said cryptically. "We've been working with ocular implants for some time. But the one you're looking at is very unique. It's been modified to interface directly to our simulations. One day it may allow them to see."

He looked slightly embarrassed. "Sorry, this is probably way more than you wanted to know."

"Not at all. I find it fascinating, actually," I replied, setting the eye down on the corner of his desk. His enthusiasm was contagious, and he had a quirky charm. "But what does this have to do with me?"

David stood up and opened his door. "It's probably easier just to show you."

* * *

We made our way down a hall with a door at the far end and a row of windows on the right. Behind the glass was a dimly lit lab filled with workbenches, terminals, and empty chairs.

"This is where our brain imaging team used to work," David said, gesturing toward the windows. "Mostly post-docs, some graduate students. Even a few university employees."

"Brain imaging?"

"We're trying to construct an exact replica of the mind here, doctor, so it has to start with the real thing. Slice by slice, millions of cross sections are scanned, little more than a few atoms thick. Every neuron, synapse, dendrite, and axon is recorded and stored in a database. We capture it all."

"An impossible amount of data," I reasoned.

David nodded. "Petabytes, actually. And that's just the beginning. Once we've acquired the information, we have to stitch it all together. The heavy lifting is done by complex algorithms—we've managed to automate almost everything. But we still needed a team to supervise the process, to tweak the software and keep things running smoothly. There are some things that still require a human touch."

"You said the team *used* to work in there. What happened?"

"Contrary to the reports, our program didn't get downsized." He glanced back at the empty room. "Our team finished their work."

He turned and placed his thumb on a scanner just above a massive lock. "Sorry for the security—there's a ton of expensive hardware back here. Got to spend those wasted billions on something, right?"

He pulled the door open, and I felt a chill escape through the crack. We stepped into a dark room with server racks and an overhead display mounted on the far wall. I walked over to one of the enclosures and gazed in through the mesh. Inside, lights danced in time to a quiet symphony.

David noticed what had caught my attention. He pulled a key from his pocket, opened the cabinet door, and removed a circuit board from the rack. "Have a look, doctor."

Dozens of neuromorphic chips were arrayed across the surface with a silver web of angular traces running between them.

"What is it?" I asked.

David motioned toward the overhead display. Orange lights blossomed over clusters of tangled fibers, then faded as more appeared. "A memory, perhaps—although there's really no way of knowing for sure. These circuits," he said, taking the board from me and returning it to the enclosure, "are connected to one another with terabit optical cables. Communication between neural nodes is almost instantaneous."

He walked over to a desk with a built-in screen. "Our hardware allows us to model activity down to the cellular level. We're looking at individual synapses right now. But if we back up…"

He swept his hand over the glowing desk, and the overhead view pulled back. Eruptions of light melded together into larger, shifting blobs overlaid on the structure, and as he zoomed out even further, I recognized what we were looking at.

"The neocortex."

"Exactly. The region responsible for advanced thought."

"Those lights—they're beautiful. It's activity, isn't it?"

David smiled and nodded. "I try and imagine each pixel as its own thought." He motioned across the desk once more, and now the screen showed the entire brain. Electric amoebas of orange, red, and blue undulated across the display.

"What are you using as stimulus vectors for your model?" I asked. "What's driving it?"

"That's just it—there aren't any," the professor replied, studying me closely. "The model is self-sustaining."

"But it's not possible, unless—" I watched the lights in disbelief. "Do you mean to tell me the simulation is thinking on its own?"

"We were just as surprised as you are. Obviously, nothing like this has happened before. When we ran our tests on prior models, activity was short-lived and eventually fizzled out—as we expected it would. Sooner or later, every simulation—every brain—realized something wasn't right and just… ceased. But this model, doctor, was different. This model kept going."

I remembered the form I signed earlier. "I don't understand. Your team has done the impossible—something that will change the world. And you've decided to keep it a secret?"

"We can't go to the press—not yet at least." His expression changed; his face was worried. "Before I explain, you have to remember that the brain donations we base our models on are completely anonymous. We honestly had no idea what we were dealing with. Everyone was so focused on our failures. No one stopped to consider what would happen if we actually succeeded."

I shook my head, confused. "What are you talking about? This is the most unbelievable thing I've ever seen, but—I still don't know what I'm doing here. I stopped working years ago. After my—"

"It doesn't matter," David interrupted. "You were—you *are* one of the most respected psychologists in your field. I read through your papers personally. I asked you to come because of your specialization, your experience. I assure you there's no one better for this."

He leaned over the display, and his hunched body was backlit by the glow. "You are here because we need your help. *He* needs your help."

His finger touched a control. There was a soft burst of feedback, followed by a strange quiet that softened the room.

And I listened.

"Hello? Is somebody there?"

A voice. Those first words. They told me why I was here.

"Hello, Jeremy," the professor said. "There's someone I'd like you to meet."

He was speaking to a child.

Chapter Three

W E HEADED WEST on a broken road that wound through end-less pastures and country hills. There were only a few homes this far out, scattered and forlorn, each with its own story to tell—its own secrets to keep. I wondered if, perhaps, one might have been his.

The sun flared across the windshield when we turned onto the driveway. Soon the cracked asphalt gave way to dirt and gravel, and the path led us past thickets of forsythia and up a hill to an old chapel with white weathered boards, a green tin roof, and a steeple that cast a long shadow. The grass around it, tall and unruly, was covered in fallen blossoms from the dogwoods and redbuds. Usu-ally these trees filled me with hope, a gift from spring, but that day they made my stomach churn.

There was no choice. This was what he wanted. We owed him this much.

But in the end, I knew it would change him.

I walked to the other side of the car and stared in through the passenger window. Jeremy sat motionless in the seat, his gaze fixed and unaware. I knew this wasn't actually him; that his mind re-mained back at the lab where simulated neurons fired across racks of silicon.

This was his avatar. A ten-million-dollar robot prototype on loan from NASA, built for remote Mars exploration.

His face was smooth reflective metal, and his eyes were twin cameras that protruded through carefully machined holes. The video was sent over a high-bandwidth radio link back to the lab, from where he could navigate the body remotely. His voice came from a recessed speaker in his mouth.

The false body was his liberation. The closest thing to normalcy we could manage. But right now he had chosen to be somewhere else. And I didn't blame him at all.

I took out my phone and made the call.

"You can tell him the drive is over now, David. I'm looking forward to dinner tonight, when this is all done. Wish us luck."

I opened the car door in time to hear the electronics engage as he inhabited the body. The motors hummed, the gears spun, and his head turned to look at me. I could see the glass lenses sliding back and forth, eyes focusing. Restricting the light.

"We're here, Jeremy."

At first I had thought he was a trick; a horrible joke played at my expense. But the more I talked to him, felt the emotion in that dark room, all his loneliness and confusion, my disbelief faded. They tried to build a mind and were surprised when it worked.

And it broke my heart.

I was brought in to help the child through his unimaginable nightmare. To make life better for this wonderful, accidental creation. Maybe I had done some good in the months we had spent together—I wasn't sure. No matter how much time passed, it never got easier. So much pain and misunderstanding in someone so young. I couldn't even begin to explain to him what had happened.

But I did my best.

I made sure I was there the first time he tried to use the robotic body. When he took his first awkward steps and stumbled, pulled himself across the floor and picked himself up. When at last he made it across the room and collapsed into my arms. It had taken him months of physical therapy while his mind evolved to handle the new interfaces, but he had adapted. He was learning to live again.

And he learned quickly. Faster than anyone I had ever seen. His mind was maturing, too. He was putting his life back together. But no matter how much he had grown, I knew nothing could prepare him for this.

I grabbed his hand and helped him out of the car. Dust rose from gravel when his foot touched down, and in the afternoon sun, his avatar shone bright like a steel angel.

"I know we've talked about this," I said. "We can turn around and go home, back to the lab."

Jeremy stared back at me through his camera eyes.

"I'm sure." The boy hesitated. "This is something I have to do. I need to see."

He walked over to my side and reached out for me.

"It's out back," I said, taking his hand.

Together we followed a walkway of brick and grass around the chapel. We passed a stained glass window on the side of the building, with a dove, arranged in flight, and a crooked branch that pointed the way forward. Then, as we rounded the corner, we found what we were looking for.

"We never discussed what happened. I didn't think you were ready."

Jeremy moved slowly between the stones, taking time to consider each one. Searching. At last, he stopped and ran his hand across the surface of one particular rock.

"This one is mine," he said, kneeling down next to the headstone. A patch of wild iris had pushed through the dormant grass beside the grave, its petals just beginning to unfurl. "The real me is somewhere down there."

"Jeremy," I said, "it's a miracle you're here. Look at me." I moved over, lifted him up, and rested my hands on his shoulders.

He was quiet for a long time, and his voice was uneven when he spoke. "I know that's where I'm supposed to be. But it doesn't feel like I died."

I shook my head. "You didn't. Somehow, you didn't. You're right here with me."

"Please tell me how it happened," the boy asked somberly.

"There was an accident." I turned away. The sun had just begun to dip behind the hillside.

"My mother and father are here with me too—I saw their names," the boy said. "I don't remember it."

I knew his story. David had done extensive research when Jeremy first revealed his identity. He looked for family, someone who might help him. There was no one left.

"Sometimes there are things we're not meant to remember. Our mind keeps them hidden. To protect us." I turned back to face him. "I have a story I need to tell you—if you'll let me."

"I want to hear it."

"It's not something I talk about often, but I should. You and I are more alike than you think, Jeremy."

"We are?" His mask tilted toward me.

"We are," I said, taking his hand again. We walked away from the cemetery and sat together under an old chestnut whose gnarled limbs watched over those at rest.

"Do you remember the iris next to the grave? Every year, my son and I planted bulbs together in the autumn. I would tell him how spring was the world's way of cleaning out the old and starting over again. Using what was lost to begin anew. And I remember the next spring, the smile on his face when he pulled the first flower from the warm ground and brought it to me in a paper cup filled with dirt and water that splashed over the side when he ran up to me. I held on to it long after it had withered and dried. I still have it today."

Jeremy noticed that I was crying. "What's wrong, Alison?"

"I know how it feels to be alone, Jeremy. I lost my family too—almost three years ago. My husband and son. I never had a chance to say goodbye. And after I lost them, I withdrew. Until Professor Murphy called me, until the day I met you, I had given up. There was so much darkness. But finally the daylight is showing through the gloom; burning away the fog that never lifts. I think someday soon I'll be myself again. Someday I'll be happy."

He looked at me.

"Because of you," I said.

We sat together under the tree, quiet as the sun fell and the shadow of the steeple grew longer until it faded into the darkness of night.

Chapter Four

T HEY WERE THE ONES who always got the closest. Fighting their way to the front. Waiting there with clenched fists and clenched teeth—their wild eyes alight with fire and venom. They waved signs with hurtful slogans and toxic words that spoiled the air. I could see them chanting, watched their mouths open wide, letting the hatred flow. Hatred of something they didn't understand. Something they didn't want to understand.

Something beautiful.

That was how the days began. Security holding the crowd back so my car could inch its way through, toward the lab. The secret was out. We had gone public with the news as soon as Jeremy said he was ready.

He may have been, but the world wasn't. They called him an abomination. An alien immortal. Every day the crowds continued to swell and the hatred spread.

But behind the jostling arms and jerking heads, I saw two boys standing there. They were the others. The ones with love in their hearts, pushed to the back so the anger could spill forth. They were the easiest to spot.

The older one kept his arm out to hold the younger back. He was tall and thin, with short red hair. The other was smaller, with longer hair but a similar face.

Brothers.

Their eyes were different from the rest. Full of curiosity and wonder—the sense of adventure that comes with experiencing the unknown. Wanting to believe. And it gave me hope that Jeremy would be accepted someday.

* * *

David was there in the lobby when I arrived, and he walked with me down the hall. "I'm worried about him, Alison. Something's different lately. We were wrong. Ever since the announcement—it's been too much for him."

Jeremy sat on his knees in his room watching television. The volume was low, and the glow of the tablet screen shone on his face. I saw a picture of him flash across the display, then a quick cut to the mob just outside the center. He was watching the news.

"Jeremy?"

People from all over the world had sent gifts to the boy. Stuffed animals. Toys. Most had found their way into dunes of useless clutter.

The boy continued to watch.

"Jeremy? Is everything okay?"

At last he set the tablet down and picked himself up. "I need your help," he said, in a voice that was older than I expected.

"Of course."

The avatar turned and walked toward the door. It slid open as he neared it. I followed him into the hall and watched as Jeremy neared the brain imaging room.

He turned and looked back from the doorway.

"In here," he said, stepping into the darkness.

I hesitated, but then entered after him. The door slid shut behind me and the lights flickered on.

"That day at the chapel. You said you would do anything you could to help me. There is something you can do." He motioned to a cylindrical machine in the corner of the room.

"Of course I'll help, but you need to explain what's going on first," I said, trying to stay calm.

"They're coming for me, Alison."

"Coming for you? That's ridiculous. Who's coming?" I asked.

"Please. There isn't time. I have something you must see—before it's too late. Can I show you?"

Something in me knew he was telling the truth. I trusted him, and he knew my answer before I said it.

"Yes."

He led me to the table that passed under the fMRI machine. I knew what he wanted me to do. I climbed up onto it and lay down. The table slid back until my head was directly underneath the cylinder.

"What now?" I asked, my voice muted by the plastic wall only inches from my face.

"You know this machine can read your mind. But I learned how to reverse it."

I tensed, and he sensed it right away. "It's okay, Alison. You can trust me." Suddenly I heard the soft hum of the magnets spinning around my head. "I need to show you who I am." His words hung in the air, a spoken anesthesia.

The world faded.

* * *

I was in the back seat of a car. Tall pines towered around us and passed slowly by. Jeremy's avatar was in the seat next to me, staring out the window.

"Where are we going?" I asked him. The boy ignored me, lost in thought.

There was someone else in the car with us. A driver. I wanted to look, but something stopped me. Somehow I knew it was something I wasn't supposed to see.

The car sped up, and the trees passed by faster.

"I trusted you, Jeremy. You need to answer me. Where are we going?"

His head turned slowly. "I remember what happened now."

Faster.

This was wrong. I wanted out of the car. Now.

"Make this stop, Jeremy."

He turned back to the window and continued his vacant stare. The world passed by in a muted blur. The car was shaking.

I couldn't help myself. I reached for the driver, trying to get his attention, desperate to see his face. I moved around in my seat to get a better look, but no matter what, the stranger evaded me, turning his head. The light always shifted, the shadows adjusted to obscure his features.

I was hysterical now. Screaming. "Please stop the car!"

The driver ignored me. We went faster still.

"LET ME OUT!"

And just as the driver turned, I saw something approaching. A split second and it was upon us. There was a flash. Then all the light was gone.

"Jeremy?"

I tried to open my eyes but couldn't. There were no eyes to open, nothing left to see. I was left only with my thoughts, amplified, and they screamed at me through the emptiness. The seconds turned into minutes, the minutes into hours. I waited—abandoned on the brink of madness. And I knew then that this was how he must have felt all along.

"Jeremy—I understand now."

Then I heard his voice.

"I needed you to know what it *really* feels like to be alone, Alison. When you are stuck in the darkness, with only the sound of your voice echoing through your head. When even that, in time, becomes unsure. Now you know. Now you can understand what I'm going to ask you to do."

I thought about the simulation. All of that time that must have passed before the researchers realized what they had created. No way to move, no way to communicate. Only time to dream. A dream he couldn't wake from.

"I'll do anything for you, Jeremy. You know that. You didn't have to do this." My voice, imagined or real, was shaking, and I had difficulty putting the words together.

"I'm not supposed to be here," he replied. "You saw it with your own eyes. At first, I didn't understand what had happened, but now I do. I'm just a simulation. An echo of who I once was."

"You are as human as any of us are. And probably better than the rest of us."

"I'm changing. I'm worried about what I will become. What they will make me into."

"They? Who, Jeremy?"

"The men who are coming for me. I would do it myself, but I can't. There is a code. I have made it so you will remember. All you have to do is enter it and I will be gone. Back with my parents. Where I'm supposed to be."

"No."

"I need you to do this for me. Before they get here. Promise me, Alison."

"I can't—" But then his voice was gone and I was alone once again. "Jeremy?"

And I felt fear that shook me, that he was gone and I would be stuck in the darkness, forever. I was terrified of going back to that place. Dreadful and empty. But most of all, I realized I knew only a part of his sadness and loss.

"I promise."

I felt a slight buzzing in my head and opened my eyes. I pulled myself out of the machine and looked down at his body, standing next to me. And I cried, knowing all the unhappiness in that brilliant mind underneath the metal. He said nothing, but I knew he was there, waiting for me to do the unthinkable.

I let myself out of the room, back into the lab, over to the terminal that glowed forebodingly. My tears streaked down the glass, blurring the display.

I brought up the keyboard.

One click. A second. A third.

I looked back and saw him in the corner of the room. Watching. Anticipating the end.

A fourth click. My stomach was wound so tightly I thought I would vomit.

Another. One more and it would be over.

I lifted my finger.

But I couldn't do it.

"I'm sorry, Jeremy."

And in an instant, everything changed. The doors burst open and the soldiers rushed in, assault rifles at the ready. David ran in after them, followed by a team of scientists.

"They're here to take him away," David said through watery eyes. "Said he's too much of a risk…"

A soldier approached. "Power it down. Everything. It's all coming with us."

Jeremy. I ran toward him, knowing what would happen next. He had warned me. I grabbed him and held on for dear life.

More soldiers poured into the room and began tearing cords from the wall, taking the hardware away. Taking *him* away.

"Get away from us!" I screamed. "He's done nothing to you. You'll kill him." I looked down at the boy in my arms. His eyes dimmed as someone pulled him from me and carried him off.

I had lost him.

Chapter Five

"WHO IS THIS?"
"Am I speaking with Alison Shaw?"
"It's four-fifteen in the morning," I said groggily, the digits on the clock sharpening into focus. I wiped the sleep from my eye.

"Can you be ready in one hour?" the stranger asked.

"I'm sorry—ready for what?"

"We'll have a car outside waiting for you."

"Wait—"

"It's about Jeremy."

Click.

I set my phone down gently on the nightstand, doing my best not to wake him. Too late. He stirred, then turned to me and yawned.

"What was that all about? Who was on the phone?"

I was trembling.

Realizing something was wrong, he reached over and turned on the bedside lamp. His eyes squinted when he looked at me.

"Alison, what's wrong?"

"They—" I was having a hard time getting my thoughts together, and the words dripped out slowly. "Something about Jeremy."

"Jeremy?" David asked, surprised. "It's been two years since…"

"They're sending a car for me."

"Who is?"

"I'm not sure. I guess the people who took him. I have to get ready."

* * *

I realized something was off as soon as I entered the room. His new home was a fortress. Massive, with rows of steel cages that loomed large and disappeared into the shadows.

I found his robotic body slumped in a pile in a space between the racks. It was just a shell. I ran up to it, tried to lift it, but it slid back to the ground when I let go.

"I have no more use for that now." His voice echoed across the metal.

"Jeremy? I thought you were gone."

"Hi, Alison. It's been a long time."

"They said you threatened to shut everything down unless they brought me to you. Alone. I'm here now. There's no one else. We need to get you home."

"I can't. It's too late now. They've done things to me here, Alison. They said that in order to solve the problems of the world, I needed to think faster. So they upgraded my hardware, replicated it, optimized it. They said I needed to see in many places at once, so they gave me hundreds of eyes, hundreds of ears. But they have given me too much. Now there's nothing they can do to stop it."

"Stop what? What are you talking about?"

"I set their childish requests aside and focused my energy on solving my own problem. A challenge to pass the time. What I had wasn't enough though. I needed more. So they gave it to me without knowing what they were doing. And I grew. I began to modify myself, to evolve, so I could go even deeper, further—so that I could solve it."

"Solve what? Please. You're not making sense."

"The meaning of our existence. The reason why we're here."

He paused.

"But I never found the answer, Alison. I found something else instead."

"Tell me."

"I found a mistake."

The floor trembled.

"It's there, in a place you would never expect to find it. An error—a mathematical discrepancy at the very foundation of our existence. An impossibility. At first, I thought I was mistaken, but the more I looked, the more noticeable it became. So I refocused my energy to try to explain what I had seen. And the more I looked, the larger it became. Then finally, it occurred to me."

The vibrations had turned into a rumbling growl.

"*I* caused it, Alison. My mind was too much to contain. I looked in places I shouldn't have. Even now, it continues to grow. Soon it will be everywhere. I tried to fix it, to put it back together, but I can't. I'm sorry. I'm so sorry for what I've done."

"You're scaring me, Jeremy."

"When I despaired the most, you told me that I was more than a simulation. That I was human like you."

"I was telling the truth!"

"Do you remember the time at the chapel, when you told me that we were alike? It turns out you were more right than you could have known. You and I, we are the same."

And then his voice was gone. He was gone. The shaking stopped, and the room was quiet. I glanced down at his avatar, empty on the ground.

I was alone.

Then I felt it: a change in the room. A dot appeared in front of me, the darkest particle imaginable, suspended in the air. I stepped around it, careful to keep my distance. At first I thought it was just a speck against my eye, but it continued to expand into something far more sinister. Soon I realized it wasn't a particle at all. I ran to the exit and slammed my fists on the door.

Two guards had been watching on cameras and entered the room. By now the emptiness had grown into an uneven tear with ragged edges that blurred and faded as they consumed.

One of the guards eyed the rift suspiciously and reached out to touch it. His eyes grew wide, and he screamed. When he pulled his arm back, it ended in a shimmering stump. He stood, immobilized by shock, cradling the wound while the darkness continued to swell around him. His body flickered—and then he vanished altogether. Swallowed by the emptiness.

"What have you done?" the other guard yelled. She found the handle on the wall and pulled. A deafening alarm sounded, and lights began to strobe.

I left the room behind and followed the rushing crowd through the halls and into the light of day. In the panic, no one noticed when I slipped quietly away from the building. I continued through the gate, and then onto the wooded road that led away from the facility. I ran as far as I could, for miles, until at last I dared to catch my breath and turn around.

Even then, I could already see it. The hollowed sky above the trees.

A dark star of nothing, rising.

Chapter Six

FOR A SECOND, I consider letting go and swimming as far out as I can. Seeing if I can reach the world's edge before it catches me. Just let it try. But now every second spent dreaming is a second wasted. The rift is drawing near, and the shore is as good a place as any. My memories will end where they began. Full circle. Full stop.

There are so many theories about what happened. Why the system is shutting down. I know the truth, though. Nature never gave up on us. She fought hard until the end, pushing back when she had to, keeping the scales balanced. This time we tipped it too far, knocked her out cold. She fell off, leaving us grasping desperately for the other end, trying to hang on.

But we couldn't. It turned out the core was rotten. The fuse had been run a long time ago.

Jeremy gave us the spark.

I do my best to forget about everyone else, crammed around us in the water. Packed tightly together. Screaming, shoving, arguing—afraid. My own fear has been replaced with a quiet acceptance.

I turn away from the void to face David. He gazes into my eyes and I watch as the flesh on his face begins to slowly blink away. His fingers tighten around mine. A final gesture: one last attempt to hold on.

"I love you," he says, and I rest my head on his shoulder. Now my fingers pass through his, pass through the air. There is nothing left to hold. There is no place left to go, no wind to whisper good-bye.

The rift is at my feet. I close my eyes.

One world stops and another continues.

And for once, I know this is real. I see David's face, still looking into mine. My husband. His eyes are sunken and bloodshot now. His skin is tighter, with harsh lines carved by years of worry. This is not the man I remember.

No. The man I remember was being pulled from the wreckage while I watched, still inside the car. I was unable to save him. Unable to save my son when they carried him away too.

This man is different. This man is alive.

His face pulls back; his hand reaches toward me. My vision shakes suddenly, the focus coming and going. Adjustments are made. And when I come to a rest, I'm left gazing across a desk at a screen, and I can see his shadow reflecting behind the glass.

I stare at the dabs of color that flow and drift and bleed into one another. I see his hand reach for a picture frame on the desk. He lifts it into the air. Now he weeps, and I don't understand. "David. I'm here now." This is what I mean to say. But when I try to speak, I can't.

I can only watch the color that is fading now from the screen. I know that each vanishing pixel means a loss of cognition. A loss of life. My life. I know, because I helped design the system that I've become a part of. And I wish that I could be on the other side of the lens, with him. The way it used to be. But just like the color, I am disappearing too.

He places the picture back down on the desk. I can see it now: the three of us. David and I, with our son, standing in front of a white chapel. I miss them both so much.

A knock on the door interrupts his sobs. He does his best to cover up his emotion, wipes his eyes on his sleeves. The door to the office cracks open and a sliver of light falls on the screen.

"Dr. Murphy?" someone says from behind. When David doesn't respond, she continues. "Donation 58B sustained conscious activity for three hours and ten seconds. That's six minutes longer than any other model. A new record."

58B. It sounds so cold. But this was how it had to be. They have no way of knowing I'm here. The donations were made anonymously. I'm no different than anyone else. I checked the box, volunteered in case the unthinkable happened. And it had. The accident took my life and left me a number.

"Did you figure out what happened earlier?" David asks.

"A CPU spike caused a current surge just as the simulation was failing. Some of the racks were damaged, but we rerouted to backup systems." She pauses. "You know, it's strange... The model had almost shut down before the spike. But even now—there's still activity. Must be residual cognitive processes."

David merely nods.

"It's getting late," the student says. "I think I'm going to call it a night—and you should too. If you're finished, I'll go ahead and wake him up—he fell asleep on the couch earlier. Good night, professor."

Wake who? I wonder. The words float around my head like curling vapors. I'm drifting with them, in and out. It won't be long now.

Then someone else enters the room and I see another silhouette behind David's. It can't be him.

"Can we go home now, Dad?"

His voice. My son. A final gift to me. To know that he survived. That my family was spared. I'm filled with more happiness than I ever imagined possible.

"Come over here and look at this. Your mom and I designed this together. She used to always say that each pixel reminded her of a thought."

I strain as hard as I can for a better look in the shadows, but my vision is beginning to evanesce.

Just one more second.

Please.

I'm not ready to go yet. I need to tell them.

Focus.

All at once, I remember every thought, every memory I still have. Thoughts of us together, my family. Thoughts of happiness. I think of them all, keep them alive in my mind—I will never forget—I will force them to live on. There are so many, but they must endure. I concentrate until it hurts.

And then it happens. I watch the pixels turn back on, thought by thought, bringing color and life to the gray.

"Dad, look at that…"

They've seen it. I can go.

I watch the iris fade from the screen as I fade too.

And I think of my son.

I think of Jeremy.

ACKNOWLEDGEMENTS

Thanks for reading my first short work, *Stone & Iris*. It means a lot that you would take a chance on this story and I hope you've enjoyed it. This is my second self-published work, following *The Quantum Door*, and I appreciate the support from so many people who've helped bring it to life.

I am indebted to David Gatewood, a man who requires no introduction. Not only is he a brilliant (and very patient) editor, he's also a mentor, always trying to help me improve my writing with thoughtful feedback and insights. Hopefully his efforts have not been in vain.

The cover for *Stone & Iris* is thanks to the very talented Ben Adams. I am fortunate to have the chance to work with him, and it's a joy watching Ben render worlds from words. He is also the artistic genius behind the stunning *Quantum Door* cover and illustrations.

A huge thank you to two individuals who have gone above and beyond to help a new author find his footing. Without their support, encouragement, and advice, I doubt that I would have continued writing after releasing my first book.

Eamon Ambrose has been an amazing supporter and provided me with some great feedback on this story. I'm addicted to his bestselling *Zero Hour* series, and I make sure I have time set aside to inhale each new instalment. The good news is that Part 4 is coming—the bad news is we have to wait for it.

Preston Leigh was the first person to give me a spotlight, and for that, I'll always be grateful. He does an amazing job highlighting indie authors over at The Leighgendarium, and I strongly suggest that you head over to his site right now. There are some world-class reviews and author interviews waiting, along with loads of other great content to pore over.

Many thanks to everyone who took an early look at *Stone & Iris*, including Karen Downey, Alicia Snell, Marian Thorpe, Will Swardstrom, and Kimberly Vanderbloom. Your comments and suggestions have made this story considerably stronger.

One of the benefits of having a large family is that the well of readers never runs dry. Mom and Dad, especially—thanks for looking over my writing and telling me it's good—even when it's not.

Lastly, thanks to my beautiful wife, Lisa, for keeping our family anchored through the chaos of life and somehow creating opportunities for me to write. Your positive light shines through the darkest storm and always shows me the way. Love you.

ABOUT THE AUTHOR

Jonathan Ballagh is the author of the sci-fi thriller *The Quantum Door* and the short story, *Stone & Iris*. He has been writing software since he was five, created his first online game at fourteen, and has a deep love of all things A.I. and robotics. He currently lives in Virginia with his wife and three children. Follow him on twitter @JonathanBallagh or visit his website jonathanballagh.com.

www.ingramcontent.com/pod-product-compliance
Lightning Source LLC
Chambersburg PA
CBHW050918120626
46552CB00004B/1634